ADIRONDACK
SASQUATCH

TO MY WIFE
LYN BEAHAN

ADIRONDACK SASQUATCH

LARRY BEAHAN

COYOTE PUBLISHING OF WESTERN NEW YORK
5 DARWIN DRIVE
SNYDER NEW YORK 14226
LARRY_BEAHAN@ROADRUNNER.COM

2013

ACKNOWLEDGEMENTS

Toby Beahan, my grandson, photographed the moose on the cover of Adirondack Sasquatch. He was not able to produce a picture of a Sasquatch that was of equal quality. So Sasqui's image is left to be supplied by the reader.

My wife, Lyn, the speller and grammarian in our house, did the much-needed editing of this book.

Northside Writers provided invaluable critiques of the various editions of this story which evolved into the one you read.

My thanks to all of you who helped to produce this book and to all of you who have taken the time to read it.

Larry Beahan

Chapter 1

"What in the dickens is Sasqui up to now?" Jo Mary Tinker mused on catching a glimpse of the Sasquatch atop a distant cliff along the convoluted shore of Tinker Island. Yukon, her grey and tan mixed Siberian husky, looked where she was looking, sniffed and went back to snoozing.

The wind riffled through Jo Mary's long gray hair, flannel shirtsleeves rolled to her elbows, dungarees just covering the tops of leather boots propped on the rail of her porch. She sat in an old wooden Adirondack chair with worn canvas cushions added for comfort. This cabin and its accoutrements had served the Tinker clan for four generations. She had lived most of her sixty-seven years right here.

From high on that rocky island, she had a view west down the length of the Stillwater Reservoir toward the new Beaver River Dam. The new dam was higher than the original one built in the 1920's and had made an island of what had been the Tinker peninsula. To the north, a forest comprised of the Pepper Box and Five Ponds Wilderness Preserves stretched out before her. The Beaver River twisted and tossed as it poured spring snowmelt into the basin behind the new dam. A sizeable stretch of river now cut the Tinker Peninsula off from its ancient logging road access toward Croghan and Lowville.

Jo Mary thought half aloud, "Water's risin', Mister Sasqui. That cave of yours is goin' to be underwater soon. Are you goin' to be more sociable, Mister… and Missus Sasqui?" "Christ!" she exclaimed "I wonder how many of them there are." The thought of being outnumbered disquieted her.

Jo Mary peered through an old pair of Bushnell 7X50 marine binoculars that Uncle Todd Tinker had brought home from

Japan after his tour with the USAF. She stared at a shadow beneath an overhanging stone outcrop. She knew it to be a good-sized cave half-way up the steep cliff wall. She discovered that remote cave fifty-one years ago when she was sixteen and never revealed its existence to anyone. When she found the cave, it was in a steep ravine well back from the shoreline of the reservoir. Now the rising river waters threatened to cover the cave mouth.

"There he is," she whispered out loud. A hairy face flashed momentarily in one bright sunlit corner of the shadowy entrance. She thought, nobody believed me when I told them what I saw down there. They laughed me off, said I read too many comic books. If I had convinced them there were Sasquatch out there, they'd have gone out and killed them.

Thank God they took me for a kid with an overgrown imagination. Now I have this little patch of paradise to myself with an amazin' opportunity tossed in. I've got everything, every damn thing I need plus a Sasquatch. Nobody, not Jane Goodall, not Charles Darwin, nobody has had such a private damn laboratory. "How'd I get so lucky in my old age?" she chuckled.

Jo Mary waved at where the face had been, "Hey, Sasqui. Come on up here and sit a spell, why don't you."

Her long residence in this wild environment taught her to navigate the woods, deal with snakes, bears, white water, sub-zero weather, and gave her a certain wariness of all new contacts. She was not frightened by her recent sightings of this Sasquatch that she called Sasqui. She felt a kinship toward him since they remained the only apparent occupants of the 1000 acres of Tinker land that was above water. But she intended to be careful with him.

The cabin was sturdily built of virgin white pine logs and brought up to date inside with plasterboard and wallpaper. An electric generator and propane stove supplemented the monumental fireplace that Great Grandfather Daniel Tinker had constructed when he took the job of Lumber Supervisor for the Youtsey Lumber Company that owned a hundred thousand acres of timberland here in the heart of the Adirondack forest. After most of the timber was gone, Grampa Tinker was able to buy the Tinker land and the family stayed on farming, hunting, guiding working on the Beaver River Power Project, whatever came to hand.

There was no cellphone reception but a shortwave radio allowed communication to the outside world. The only television available arrived by DVD.

Jo Mary's brother, Jim, his wife Oliva and their one-year-old, Marcellus, were the last to leave the Tinker homestead six months before. Officer Jeff Williams of the New York State Department of Environmental Conservation warned the Tinkers that their hill-top home would soon be an island in the middle of the expanded Stillwater Reservoir. "Yes Ma'm, they dropped the lower floodgates in yesterday," he said between draws on his pipe. "The river will fill her up gradually. Be probably a few months till the generators start pumpin' kilowatts. Keep New York City bright and shiny. But if you stay here, you won't be able to use the Old Truck Road out to Croghan for long. Won't be any maintenance. It'll be either snowmobile, boat or swim for your groceries from now on."

The government officials and the whole Tinker clan could not prevail on Jo Mary to leave the place. She put her foot down, "Leave me be. I got my Winchester and an Evinrude Outboard on my Zodiac. Long as Uncle Sam keeps sendin' my Social Security checks I'll be fine. Now scat. Come back and see me for Christmas."

Jim had argued with her over and over. He threw up his hands, "You have always been bull-headed but never stupid like this."

Jim and Oliva sat down with Jo Mary one last time. They explained again that they had to get somewhere where they could earn a living and bring up Marcellus right. They hated to leave her all alone. They urged her to join them. But Jo Mary would not budge. Finally, Jim said, "Alright, you're my big sister, your mind's made up and I got to admit, you usually come up smellin' like a rose. So, you go for it."

"I hear you, honey. I'll be careful and you take care of yourself and Liva and the little tyke," she said wiping away a tear. "Come back and see me once in a while. Give me a half hour notice and I'll bake you an apple pie."

Jim said, "I'll talk to Shorty John about keepin' an eye on you and you always got the shortwave. Buffalo's not that far. If things ain't working out, give me a call. Don't be a stranger. You come see us too. Hear?"

They pecked each other on the cheek and hugged. Then, in the Zodiac, Jo Mary ferried the little family across the swelling Beaver River to their Ford 150 on the Old Truck Road.

Jo Mary crossed back to be alone with her hairy reclusive friends and her old dog, Yukon.

Chapter 2

Two weeks had passed. There was still snow in the woods. There was no sign of black flies yet. The Beaver River continued to tumble and churn as it began to fill the Stillwater Reservoir to its expanded new proportions. Jo Mary and Shorty John had made their annual trek to the Arts and Crafts Festival at Old Forge. Shorty did about 40% of his annual craft business there. Jo Mary showed three of her paintings and sold them all. She won second prize in the "Wildlife" category for a buckskin painting of Yukon frozen in predatory alertness staring at a loon that was poised to dive. A photographer from *Adirondack Magazine* snapped a photo of it and promised to send Jo Mary a clipping.

This morning, Jo Mary stood before the screen door of her cabin porch, a half-finished cup of coffee in one hand as she stared out across the waters of the reservoir. "Damn, I miss company at breakfast," she said. "That little tyke Marcellus was starting to turn into a person. I'd swear, the one time, he called me, 'Jo Mary.' I've gone off timber cruising alone for a week at a time and never felt lonesome. Travelin' in the woods you have something to do. I suppose I can keep on paintin' for Shorty John's tourists, but there's got to be more. The damn Sasquatches don't even come and visit. Christ, I thought I'd like peace and quiet, but this is overdoin' it."

Now she regularly spoke her thoughts out loud to the dog, Yukon. She remembered with a smile how, two Christmases ago, during a cold dry spell, this dog wandered into the gravelly space in front of the cabin, tongue hanging out, skinny, coat bedraggled, a Yukon Territory brass license tag clinging to a leather collar around his neck. Jo Mary set him out a bowl of milk and that apparently persuaded him to make this place home. His genetic origins were not immediately obvious. Jo Mary said, "I believe he's about half Siberian husky and half junkyard dog."

Jim differed. He said, "That critter looks lean and mean enough to be mostly wolf."

Jo Mary countered, "Well, maybe he ain't so pretty. How would you look if you escaped from a junkyard up in the Yukon and had to walk all the way from Dawson or Whitehorse? Yukon, that's what I'll call him, Yukon."

On this particular morning, Yukon sprawled in the sun on the cabin's front porch. His right ear pricked up in recognition of being addressed by Jo Mary but otherwise he did not stir until she strode over to him. "Yukon, you ever think of learnin' how to play gin rummy?"

With that overture, Yukon wagged his tail and rolled on to his back for a belly rub. Jo Mary obliged. "OK, OK, we'll play your game for now." But Yukon seemed distracted. With his head inverted, he kept glancing over his shoulder, taking distracted sniffs. He stayed on his back, clearly struggling between curiosity and the enjoyment of the sensation induced by Jo Mary's fingers. Jo Mary looked into the forest in the direction of his interest.

"My God, what is that?" she whispered to Yukon, who was by then up on all fours with his back arched and teeth bared, ready to charge. "Shh, down Yukon, stay down," she commanded, still in a whisper.

They had both seen a large dark figure dart gracefully from behind the trunk of an ancient hemlock to the concealment of a patch of brush on a low rise fifty yards to the left of the cabin porch. Jo Mary took Yukon by his collar and backed with him through the screen door into the cabin. She reached over the door for one of the two rifles hanging there. She touched Grampa Tinker's single shot Sharps 50 caliber, then selected her own deer rifle, a thirteen shot Winchester 38. Working the action to move a shell into the chamber she moved to the edge of the front window where she could see the rise but remain concealed herself. She whispered to the now cowering Yukon, "Take her easy. I'll take care of this. One way or the other, I got it covered," she reassured herself as much as she did Yukon.

"Now, unless we were both hallucinatin', there is a real live Sasquatch hidin' behind that pile of dirt. What in hell do you think he wants, company or did he come to eat us for his breakfast?"

Let's try the old milk trick. It worked pretty good on you." Jo Mary poured two quarts of reconstituted powdered milk into a bucket. With her Winchester at the ready, Yukon close behind, she carried the bucket about halfway to the rise. She set it down and walked carefully backward till she and Yukon were back indoors. For several hours they kept a watch on the rise, occasionally checking the other approaches to the cabin by making rounds of the windows.

The sun gradually set behind the dense second growth and lit up forest greenery, surrounding the reservoir in a warm yellow light. Shadows lengthened and darkness covered the silent water. Stars and moon appeared shedding their pale light on the scene and illuminating the galvanized bucket.

Jo Mary's stomach grumbled and she was sore from squatting at the window so long. She said to Yukon, "I'm hungry, how about you?"

Yukon nuzzled her shoulder. So Jo Mary leaned the Winchester against a kitchen chair, warmed up the remains of a venison stew, sliced some bread and made herself a pot of coffee. She poured half the stew into a plastic bowl for Yukon. With a sigh, she sat down at the kitchen table where she had shared so many meals with the Tinker clan. She spoke to Yukon, "What a wonder it is. I wish all the folks could have seen this. We got us a Sasquatch…unless he's got us."

"Might as well say grace, Yukon." She folded her hands and said, "Bless us, oh Lord, and these, thy gifts…" Yukon gobbled his share.

When both had finished, they returned to their watch. The bucket was gone. "You see that?" Jo Mary said to Yukon. "He's interested." Yukon stared intently out the window.

"Question is, does he want to be friends or what?"

Jo Mary bolted the cabin's front and rear doors and closed and barred the interior shutters that Daniel Tinker had crafted back when neighbors included bears, drunken lumberjacks and sometimes fugitives from the law.

She and Yukon sat by an upstairs window till very late when Jo Mary gave a yawn and said, "OK Sasqui, do your damndest. I'm goin' to get some sleep." She threw herself on the quilt covering her steel frame bed and promptly fell asleep. Yukon yawned a little yawn and joined her.

Chapter 3

Jo Mary woke with a start. The early spring sun was well risen. She reached for the rifle leaning against her bedstead and stepped to the bedroom window. Yukon, still on the bed, stretched and then seemed to remember the strange smells and sights of the previous evening as he reached her side in a bound.

"Sasqui brought his dinner bucket back. Don't suppose he washed it," she chuckled. Yukon stared.

"Let's go over there and see what's what. No, let's get some breakfast first and check what we can see out the back windows before we stick our necks out. Sasqui must be kind'a desperate to be reachin' out at us like this. We'll just take our time and do this thing careful like. OK?"

About an hour later, after a wash, a fresh flannel shirt and reconnoitering the premises, Jo Mary and Yukon ventured out the front door. Jo Mary rested her 38 comfortably in the crook of her right arm. They walked to where the bucket had been returned. It was empty of milk but a half dozen Trillium blossoms decorated the container. "Will yah look at that," Jo Mary exclaimed. "Now that is sweet, Yukon. How come you don't bring me flowers?"

Yukon sniffed about warily, never straying far from Jo Mary.

So it became a daily routine that Jo Mary would leave a supply of food; bread, milk, oatmeal mush, fry cakes and the like each night. In the morning she would find the food gone and a gift of flowers or colorful stones. She caught only fleeting glimpses of the creature with whom she had established this trade.

Then one morning on the porch Jo Mary said, "Yukon, what do you think? Should I give you a rest and try paintin' a picture of our big hairy friend?" Yukon nuzzled her leg and Jo Mary scratched that good spot just above his tail. Shorty John had given her an old steel snow shovel missing its wooden handle,

"Paint me a moose put him in front of some High Peaks or maybe Avalanche Lake. Some city slicker pay us fifty bucks for it. We split."

But Jo Mary got out her paint tubes. She daubed on her pallet black and brown and a bit of bright orange for the face, and green and blue for forest and water. She put the shovel up on the porch rail and leaned it against one of the posts supporting the roof. Soon the shovel bore sky, water, forest and, in the foreground, a tall hulking figure with a thick black coat of body hair, long muscular arms and lively facial features. It looked about one third bear, a third orangutan, and a third human being. The creature wore a broad grin on its orange face. In his extended right hand he held Trillium blossoms.

Yukon watched Jo Mary work. When she tried to pull his head up on to her lap for a closer look he pulled away with an uncharacteristic growl. "What's the matter Yukon? You jealous? "

By that evening, Jo Mary had finished this Sasquatch painting and it made three pieces she had ready for sale. She radioed Shorty John and he agreed to have his son, Little, check out her Chevy pickup parked behind his store and drive it to meet her at the beach in front of the Stillwater Hotel.

The next morning, early, she put her new paintings carefully into a canvas backpack, surrounded them with extra clothes and put a lunch and two canteens of water in the pack's outside pockets. Shouldering the load and carrying the now ever-present Winchester, she and Yukon made their way down the old road to the water's edge. The Tinker fishing dock floated in a cove of gradually rising water. The dock was built ingeniously to rise and fall with the changing levels of the reservoir. It only required adjustment of its mooring ropes every few days to keep it in place. The family's inflatable Zodiac with its 175-horse power Evinrude engine floated alongside the dock.

Jo Mary and Yukon climbed aboard and soon were noisily bouncing through the rapidly moving river toward the tiny village at the southwest end of the Stillwater Reservoir. The sky was clear blue and the sun promised a preview of summer heat. On the way they had a look at the fresh white concrete of the new dam and water pouring through its partially closed spillway. Yukon stood in the bow, nose pointed into the wind like a hood ornament on a Jaguar. When they neared a deserted corner of the beach Yukon made a leap that landed him high and dry. Jo Mary drove the rubber craft firmly up onto the sand, shut down the engine and then followed him ashore with the Dacron bow line in her hand. She noted that the old buildings close to the shore had been torn down or moved away. The hotel itself was raised up on piers.

Little John's gargantuan 6 foot 7 inch frame, topped by a tall black Stetson set squarely on his head Indian-style, rose from the shade of Jo Mary's ten-year-old Chevy pickup. He gave Yukon a quick scratch behind an ear and strode forward to take the line from Jo Mary and pulled the boat well up on the beach. He fastened the line to a maple tree just above the new high-water mark. Jo Mary went back aboard for her Danforth anchor and a second line.

When the boat was secure, Jo Mary and Little shook hands. She said, "Much obliged for comin' down here to pick me up."

"I'm pleased to be of service ma'm," he replied with a mock salute, "Pa wouldn't have it any other way. He has been worrying about you out there all by yourself." He helped her load her things into the back of the truck as Yukon sniffed at the tires.

Little John got the name Little when, for a very few years, he was the youngest and, in fact, the littlest of Shorty John's six boys. So he got called Littlest John and eventually that shortened to Little John. The name stuck for the fun of it when he overtook the entire clan in height. Everyone made sure they smiled when they addressed him that way.

In forty-five minutes they arrived at the John family's former dairy farm on the edge of the village of Croghan. Jo Mary pulled the truck into the gravel parking lot beside a long low building constructed of logs. A professionally painted sign stretched across the building's front, depicting, from the shoulders up, a Mohawk warrior wearing the traditional three-eagle-feather buckskin cap. The sign announced "Shorty John's Mohawk Museum and Trading Post." An arrow penetrated the length of the words. A farmhouse stood several yards behind the Trading Post and a modern barn-sized garage had replaced the barn Shorty tore down when he left the dairy business for the mercantile world.

The Trading Post was furnished with a verandah of unfinished pine. Shorty had heard Little toot the horn down the road. He burst out the wide swinging double doors and down the flagstone steps to greet them. His movements were quick, though limited by a gait between a waddle and a limp. He wore a printed red handkerchief tied in a band around his head, a broad welcoming grin on his face and carried a can of ice cold Coca Cola in each hand. "Hello, Missy. Come sit in the sun," he said.

Jo Mary raised a hand in greeting. "Hi Shorty, that does look good," she said, taking the drink and easing onto a wooden bench alongside the flagstone approach to the Trading Post.

Shorty sat down beside her and chuckled, "How you like it out there on that island? That's a dirty trick the government playin' on you. Treatin' you like a Injun."

"Ain't that bad," she smiled taking a swig of Coke.

"You come over to supper Sunday, week. My Missus cookin' up big feed. Fry bread, corn mush, venison; real home cookin'. All the cousins comin'. How about it?"

Little ducked to accommodate his six-foot-seven-inches as he strode up onto the porch to retrieve a grape soda from the cooler by the front door. He returned to stand leaning against the truck and said, "It's going to be a good feed, you better come along."

Jo Mary smiled and answered, "What can I bring?"

"Bring yourself. Your company be fine. What have yah got in the bag? Somethin' to make us some money?"

"Couple more paintin's," she said, loosening the straps and lifting the snow shovel bearing Sasqui's image free of its packing.

Once he got a look at it, Shorty's eager expression changed to a frown. He let out a grunt. "What's that thing? I seen him. Come down out of the back country. Goin' after my stock. I put a slug in 'em. Looked dead. Couldn't decide should I scalp 'em or eat 'em.' Thing woke up, charge me. Run over me like a bull moose. Ever since this leg no good, ache," he said angrily massaging his right leg.

Little leaned over to squint at the image. "That is a Sasquatch."

His father barked, "Little, get my Sharps 50 caliber."

Chapter 4

Little John squinted at his father, rolled the last of his grape soda around in the bottom of the can, then threw his massive head back to finish off the drink. Jo Mary let out a snort of forced laughter, "Shorty, you want to come over to my place, lookin' for phantoms and throwin' fifty-caliber chunks of lead around? I don't think so. Ain't no Big-Foot-Sasquatch around my place. I copied that picture out of *Field and Stream Magazine.*" She stood up, slapped her knee and gave Shorty's shoulder a shove. "For-cryin'-out-loud, I had you goin' there, didn't I?"

Rocking back with her shove, the old Indian looked square into Jo Mary's eyes, "You got that from *Field and Stream*? When? I been getting' *Field and Stream* since 1957. I don't see it."

"Maybe it was *National Geographic*. I got that moose you liked so much from one of my daddy's old stash of magazines. He loved those outdoors magazines. Had so many saved up I had to burn them to make room when Liva had baby Marcellus. The Sasquatch story was a great piece. I got a real kick out of it. I'll never forgot the look of the poor thing in their picture, kind of scared, like all he wanted was to be left alone. That's how I painted him, too. Felt sorry for the poor feller."

"Don't you go feelin' sorry for those nasty critters, Missy. Look what that one done to me." Shorty got up and exaggerated into a hobble the limp that his arthritic right hip had given him. He lunged from the bench over to the crude wooden porch rail.

Little smiled saying, Pa, better cut that out. Somebody will take you for Hop-a-long Cassidy."

Jo Mary shuddered inwardly and grinned hard to cover the shudder. The image of hunting parties tracking the harmless companion with whom she shared Tinker Island filled Jo Mary with dread and sadness. Her dream of an opportunity to protect and learn about Sasquatch, even possibly a whole Sasquatch family, was being swallowed up by the image of benign orange faces exploding in terror.

These quiet gentle creatures whose only offenses were that they looked different and wanted to live apart might be hunted into extinction because she had revealed their existence. I cannot let this happen, she swore to herself.

Little broke the impasse, "You still need the old blunderbuss, Pa?"

"Ain't no blunderbuss. That Sharp's fed your family lot of moose steak," Shorty John said and then nodded at Jo Mary and grinned speculatively, "Clean 'em up just in case."

"You old faker," Jo Mary said a bit too shortly. "You don't believe me? I ever tell you a lie?"

"Not up to now."

"I swear this picture is made-up imagination. Why nobody has ever actually proved these things exist. That article was a joke."

"Sasquatch ain't a joke to Mohawk people. We been here long time. Oldtimers call them Stone Giants. They hang around out of sight. Bad medicine, bad luck, hurt people. Look at this leg," he motioned to his bad leg again. "I seen him."

Jo Mary finished up her Coke and nodded thoughtfully. Then said, "Guess I'd feel that way too if a Sasquatch beat up my leg like that. But I'm not worryin' about it until I actually see one of those critters. And that's the last time I'm goin' to let my imagination go wild and paint another one no matter if they pay me a hundred dollars for it." Jo Mary started to slide the shovel blade with its Sasquatch image back into her knapsack.

Shorty John held her wrist in his callused fist and prevented her, saying, "I'll give you a hundred."

Jo Mary looked at his hand and warned him slow and low, "I don't like that, Shorty."

Shorty released his grip and backed away a step. Little stepped between them, saying, "Jo Mary you know he didn't mean nothing by that."

Shorty quickly changed his expression and said, "Jo Mary, we are old friends. That picture got me stirred up. I sure would like to have that picture."

Jo Mary thought quickly. I'm makin' too much out of this. Now he'll start believin' I saw the critter. So she backtracked. "Tell you what, old buddy. You can have it, since it means so much to you. Anyway, it's your shovel so you've got a right to it," and she handed the painting to Shorty.

"Thanks Jo Mary, it's a beauty," he said with a big smile. "Little, get a hundred out of the cash register."

"No, no, I can't take your money, just promise you won't be bringin' no huntin' parties over to my land lookin' to shoot no moose or a Big Foot Sasquatch.

Shorty said, "Deal," and stuck out his hand.

Jo Mary surprised him by returning his handshake with the powerful grip she developed chopping wood. She added, "And under no circumstance don't bring that moose gun cannon of yours over. We got our own 50 caliber. Grampa Dan Tinker called it his rabbit gun. I got all the protection I need.

Shorty laughed, "Missy, you remind me of your ma. She could be tough as nails or sweeter than maple syrup. Come on inside. Let me settle up for those other paintin's of yours I sold. I got a half bottle of that Courvoisier your daddy used to like and we can wash her down with Polar Bear Eskimo pies. I remember you used to like them when you was little."

Jo Mary followed Shorty into the Trading post. Little found a handful of biscuits for Yukon and gave him a welcome scratching. After an hour of business and socializing conducted amidst a collection of invaluable Iroquois artifacts and a clutter of tourist goodies, Jo Mary and Little picked up groceries at the IGA and drove back to the Zodiac. Yukon, riding in the back, enjoyed the breeze.

When they reached the boat, he leapt eagerly aboard while Little and Jo Mary loaded it up and worked it back into the water. The engine caught on the first tug of the starter cord. Jo Mary waved to Little and they roared off across the water in the direction of the Tinker dock.

The roar of the 175-horse engine drowned out all other sound as both of the boat's occupants fixed their attention on the shoreline in the distance. When the dock became distinguishable from the background of rock and earth, Jo Mary saw what appeared to be a figure standing on it. "Damn, is that the life ring on the dock rail or is someone over there huntin' Sasquatch already?" Yukon stared at the dock as well. Then the figure resolved into that of the Sasqui standing upright staring at them.

"Well, I'll be," Jo Mary exclaimed as she eased off the throttle with a twist of her hand and the Zodiac settled back into the water from its plane. "Whoa, Yukon, he is one big son-of-a-bitch. So be nice now." Yukon froze in position staring at the figure on the dock.

Jo Mary idled in the current. In the distance the Sasquatch waved an arm quietly as if motioning them to join him. "He's callin' us. Maybe he missed us," Jo Mary said.

Jo Mary, for the first time, had a steady full view of the creature. She could see his dense black covering of hair, his long arms and florid face. His face was more human than an ape's and his posture more forward than a human's. "He truly looks like he missed us, Yukon. He's like a little kid tellin' us to hurry up and come home."

Yet she was hesitant. She leaned forward squinting; her right hand on the throttle ready to gun the big Evinrude out of there.

The Sasquatch watched for a time, then stopped waving, put his big hands on his low hips and turned away disappearing in the brush behind the dock. "He's givin' us a little space to get used to him. All the same though..." she started and she finished by picking up the Winchester and pumping a cartridge into the chamber. She propped the rifle on the seat beside her and steered the Zodiac alongside the dock. Yukon waited until it was absolutely clear they were going ashore before he leapt to the dock.

Jo Mary shouldered her backpack and slung the rifle in the angle of her right arm. She and Yukon made their way up the quarter-mile road toward the house. There was Sasqui again, first a dark smudge on the porch stairs and gradually his more and more familiar face and figure, now seated on the stairs. From the corner of his broad mouth, a twig protruded and bobbed as he chewed.

"Is he smilin' at us?" Jo Mary asked, then chuckled as she rested the butt of the rifle on the gravel road and considered, does he think he's going to be a boarder or does he think he is the new landlord?

Chapter 5

Jo Mary made a megaphone with her hands and yelled at the Sasquatch, "Hey you, Sasqui, get out of there. Shoo! That ain't your place. Get out. Shoo." She waved her arms at him. Yukon joined in, barking and growling.

The Sasquatch went on nibbling his twig. The yelling and barking did not seem to have any effect on him.

Jo Mary and Yukon advanced a few paces, keeping up the noise, but to no effect. Jo Mary scratched her head, thinking, I can't trust him. He's been actin' friendly but this is strange. Sasquatch are supposed to disappear the instant anyone sees 'em, Might be like a friendly fox or raccoon. They got rabies or somethin' else wrong with 'em.

"Hate to do this," she said out loud to Yukon as she raised her rifle to her shoulder and aimed at a corner log of the cabin just a few feet from Sasqui's head, where he could see it clearly. She squeezed the trigger slowly, the rifle cracked and a splinter flew from the log.

Sasqui bolted instantly across the cabin porch and disappeared behind the cabin.

"God damn, now he'll think I mean to kill him. Damn! But I couldn't let him think he owned the place"

Yukon looked accusingly at her. "No, don't say that. I never meant to hit him, just scare him off but I may have overdid it." She looked Yukon in the eye and promised, "It's goin' to be OK honey." Yukon followed her gaze as she scratched behind his ears and with her eyes searched the cabin and the woods around it.

"Nothin' for it, I guess," she said as she opened the lever action of the rifle, automatically ejecting a spent brass casing and pumping a fresh round into the chamber. Burdened with rifle and groceries, Jo Mary started again toward the cabin. Yukon sniffed carefully a few yards in advance. They climbed the stairs and she sat the groceries on the porch table.

Yukon sniffed toward the far side of the porch. Jo Mary's eyes followed him and were caught by fresh white splinters of the far-side porch railing knocked off its posts. Jo Mary walked over to inspect the damage. She let out a low whistle. "That was a pretty solid piece of pine Grampa Tinker spiked in there. Sasqui must go three hundred pounds to tear that thing out in one yank," she said to Yukon, who was busy with his own reconnoitering.

The front door to the cabin was wide open. Grampa Tinker had not wasted much cash on big windows and what windows he installed were sunk deep into the heavy log walls. A dim beam of sunlight illuminated the interior and fell on the circular oak table in front of the fireplace. There stood the milk can she had used to feed Sasqui and in it was another bouquet of Trillium beaming in the bit of sun.

"I'll be a son-of-a-gun," she whispered. "The big old sweetheart left me flowers again. And I went and scared the ba-Jesus out of him."

Yukon came in from the porch and immediately sniffed his way into the kitchen. Jo Mary followed him. The propane refrigerator door was open. Empty containers for chocolate pudding, milk, jam, peanut butter and left-over stew were strewn about and a considerable amount of their contents was on the floor. "What a mess," Jo Mary exclaimed. "He invited himself to dinner and we interrupted him." She set the box of groceries down on the rough pine-board kitchen table and started putting the cans onto the open shelves over the cupboard. Yukon got to work on the half-spilled bowl of butterscotch pudding under the table.

There was a clattering on the front porch. Yukon's ears pricked up and he started in that direction. Jo Mary grabbed his collar with one hand and her rifle with the other and hissed, "Shhhh, he's back." She checked the rifle. The safety was still off. Sliding Yukon across the floor and into the parlor she took cover behind Grampa Tinker's Morris chair. She leveled the rifle over the chair's plaid woolen cushion. Yukon offered little resistance.

A short stout figured lurched to fill the void of the open front door.

"Halt," Jo Mary shouted with the full force of her lungs. It came out higher pitched and more tremulous then she intended. So she kept on shouting. "Halt! Halt! God damn you. Halt or I'll blow you a new asshole." The figure hesitated and Jo Mary rose up, leveling the weapon at point blank range. In rising she lost hold of Yukon's collar and he charged barking like a she-wolf with pups.

Yukon's flying leap hit Shorty John about mid-chest and knocked him sprawling back onto the porch. Jo Mary recovered from her panicky explosion and recognized her old friend Shorty. Still she kept the rifle pointed in his direction as she moved out on the porch and stood over him. "Down Yukon!" she ordered in a fierce, commanding voice now deeper and clear of tremor. The dog backed off, growling.

Shorty John blustered, "What you doin' Missy? What the hell are you doin'?" He got up on one knee, "We come over here to help you, and you put that dog on me."

Shorty retrieved his black Stetson, dusted it with his sleeve and put it back squarely on his head.

Little John's towering figure came striding across the trampled area in front of the cabin, the bulky 50-caliber Sharps suspended from his shoulder by a leather sling. "I told you Pa; 'let her know you're coming. Surprise her an' she'll be dangerous.'"

Jo Mary took a deep breath and still holding her own menacing rifle said, "What are you doin' here? Sneakin' up on me. Place is all messed up. You could have been outlaws. You scared the purple Jesus out of me."

By then she had shifted the rifle to her left hand and was holding it by the barrel. She let the butt drop to the cabin floor.

"Crack," the rifle spouted fire and lead past Jo Mary's left shoulder and through pine board cieling into the sleeping loft.. Shorty, Little, Yukon and Jo Mary all jumped back out of the way of the blast.

"Damn!" Jo Mary exclaimed.

Little had jumped into the air and bolted around the corner of the house, bumped hard into Yukon as he made for the far side of the Cabin.

"What you do that for?" Shorty yelled at Jo Mary. The crease between his grey eyebrows folded into a deep furrow.

"Jesus! Hope it didn't go through the damn roof. Don't need another damn leak. See what you made me do." Jo Mary yelled. Then she shrugged disconsolately. "Somethin' wrong with this God damn gun."

"Little, you all right?" Shorty called to his son. "Come on back. It's just an accident." Then he said to Jo Mary, "He's jumpy from bein' around all that ruckus over there."

Little returned shaking his head, "Better get rid of that gun. Let me have it."

"Give it to him, Missy!" Shorty ordered. "Give it to him before you kill yourself... or someone else."

"Nope. No thanks. It's a good gun. I'll keep it handy, thanks. Now what are you boys up to, comin' over here? We took care of all the business we had to do this afternoon."

Shorty said, "We come over to skin that Sasquatch, Big Foot, Stone Giant or whatever. Skin 'em and stuff 'em. You painted his picture exactly right, just like he looks. I seen him. Close too. Big red face. Black fur all over. Why are you hidin' him?" Shorty moved very close to Jo Mary so that if he were taller their noses would almost have touched. Jo Mary looked down at him and gave him no ground. "This is my property. You don't come over here huntin' unless I give you the OK."

"You got no posted signs, Missy. You can't keep us from shootin' anything we want here unless you post your lands,"

"You want to get locked up for trespass? I'll have Jeff Williams and the DEC on you. You'll do time over to Attica."

Little interrupted, "What's this over here? Your porch is busted. Something pretty heavy hit that porch railing going fast."

Shorty broke away from Jo Mary to look at the smashed railing. "Look like a cattle stampede through here - or maybe Stone Giant."

Little unslung the big rifle he was carrying. "Jo Mary, you sure you don't need some kind of help? We slipped over here so you wouldn't see us but when we heard you shoot we came running."

"An accident. Firing pin slipped. Just like now when I set the butt on the ground, it went off."

"That's not like you, Jo Mary. You're pretty careful with guns, way I remember."

"Ain't used to being snuck up on the way you boys done. You rattled me. I'll take it over to Pete Crump in Carthage. He knows this piece. Worked on her for my daddy."

Shorty had slipped past them into the cabin. "What this?" he yelled from the kitchen. "You didn't make this mess. You just got back." Jo Mary and Little entered the parlor from the porch as Shorty emerged from the kitchen with the   butterscotch pudding bowl in his hands.

Jo Mary took a deep breath and turned to close the front door with one hand. Then she raised the Winchester with both hands to place it carefully on its rack over the door. The rack was made of the hooves and lower joint of the feet of deer. The hide and skin had been left on to protect the rifle's finish.

Shorty tasted the pudding on a thumb he had swiped around the inside of the bowl. With the bowl in his lap, he sat down on the couch that faced the fireplace and its charred logs. Little eyed the mess in the kitchen.

Jo Mary, trying to sidestep their suspicions of a Sasquatch, said, "I don't know what has got into Yukon. He's been actin' queerly." Yukon heard his name and he looked up at her from the kitchen where he was still working on the pudding on the floor. "He's gone nuts over butterscotch puddin'. I put my stuff down on the table, open the fridge and leave him alone in here a second and look what he done."

"Bad dog," she said shaking her finger toward the kitchen. Yukon did not take that as a command to stop eating. He just licked harder.

"He did that all himself, that lazy sheep-stealin' lobo of yours? I don't think so," said Shorty looking up slyly. He had put the pudding down with a different expression, a slight tilting of his nose upward.

Jo Mary said, "Hey, why don't you help yourself to some more dessert there, Shorty? I don't care what you believe; I don't want you over here huntin' my place without I tell you to. And there ain't no Stone Giant-Sasquatch over here. Little, tell your old man he's delusional, will yah?"

"Yeah, sure," said Little. He had laid his dad's Sharps rifle on the   bear skin that served as a carpet in front of the fireplace. He himself perched his outsized frame on the edge of the ten-inch-high stone slab that provided a raised platform for the fireplace. "Pa, you're delusional. They is no Stone Giant running around over here. The lady told you so and we best take her word for it and go home." He rocked forward on the toes of his tooled leather boots and started to rise.

Shorty said, "No, no, just a minute here now, Missy. You know any dog smart enough to unscrew a strawberry jam cover or a peanut butter jar cover? That critter of yours out there getting slivers in his tongue cleanin' the kitchen floor ain't an above average dog."

Chapter 6

The Johns, father and son, helped Jo Mary clean up the spilled food and broken dishes in the kitchen. Then they went to work on the porch rail. The old rail was splintered in two and the end pieces were pulled away from the uprights so the spikes were bent and protruding. The Johns cut and trimmed a young pine to fit and nailed it neatly in place.

By the time they were finished, it was 4pm. Jo Mary came out onto the porch and scratched her gray head, "Well, thank you boys, that looks better than new."

Shorty John said, laughing, "What else you got; need a new roof maybe? We'll make you a good price."

Jo Mary said, "Yeah, take a look up there, the old place could use a new coat of moss or somethin'." She thought I can't send them away hungry. They probably did think they were protectin' me. Maybe they were. Can't really say what that old Sasqui is up to, specially now that he thinks I'm tryin' to shoot him. These boys ain't real bad. Just natural born carnivores, I guess, hunters that'll shoot anything you might eat, sell or wear. So she said, "How about some dinner? I got a big pot of chili in there hot enough to challenge even your old tonsils, Shorty and I'll mix up some butter biscuits."

"Ehm, sounds real good" said Shorty, patting his round belly. "I remember Tinker chili. It's famous. We scun out after you so quick we never did get no lunch,"

Little interrupted, "I don't know, Pa, them clouds over towards home look like we could have some weather."

Jo Mary said, "I can get it on in no time. Come on in and set a spell. I got a jug of Southern Comfort I been wantin' to split with someone and you two are the only company I'm likely to have for a while."

"You got any grape soda to go with that?" Little said raising his eyebrows and leaning solemnly forward from his great height.

"Of course I do," Jo Mary responded. "Come on in," she said with a sweeping gesture that ushered them through her front door.

Shorty said, "We'll take our chances with the weather and I'll have my Southern Comfort straight if you please." Turning to Little he whispered, "Don't know where I went wrong with your raisin'. You never learned that kind of drinkin' ta' home." Then turning to Jo Mary he muttered," Spoilin' good liquor with Grape Soda, must a learn that in the Army. I never taught it to him."

The Johns spread themselves out comfortably on either end of the sofa. Jo Mary served generous tumblers of the sweet liquor for herself and each of them and tossed Yukon a treat from her pocket. He gave up on the pudding remnants and curled up on the black bear rug in front of the fireplace to watch.

Jo Mary returned to the kitchen and came back with a can of root beer, "Sorry, Little, this is all the soda I got."

"Thank you, Ma'm; this will do fine," he said accepting the frosty can."

As evening came on, the spring air cooled quickly.

"You want me to start a little fire for you?' Little offered. "May cool off tonight."

Jo Mary nodded her assent, "Yeah, a fire would feel good."

She put the biscuits in the oven, heated the chili, and set the dining room table while Little broke up some kindling, brought in an armload of split wood. Shorty sat sipping and thinking. When the fire was ready to be lit Little slapped the pockets of his pants with a puzzled look. Shorty fumbled in the pocket of his crisp new jeans and produced a yellow plastic Bic lighter which he flipped toward his son. "What were you goin' to do, the old Injun trick rubbin' two sticks together?"

Little caught the lighter skillfully and in a moment he had the fire blazing.

"Come and get it," Jo Mary called as she set a steaming bowl of chili in the center of the great round oak dining table. They all took seats. Little shoveled tablespoonfuls of chili into his mouth as he towered over the table munching biscuits and drowning it all with soda. He never said a word though his eyes glistened and he smiled as he ate.

His father, however, took one mouthful, rolled his eyes, swallowed hard and reached for a biscuit and a glass of water. "Eyahoo," came a muffled howl. And after another swallow, "That is hot," then a pause and a gasped, "and sooo good." He brought another heaping spoonful to his mouth.

Jo Mary savored the steaming red mixture. The jalapenos brought out the sweetness of the tomatoes, the delicate essence of the green peppers, the aromatic flavor of the onions, the full fleshiness of the beef and all enhanced the soft red beans that carried and blended the flavor of the other components. Just as good as Grandma's, she thought as the spice reached into her brain and produced its warm tingling bite throughout her body.

They talked of the tourist trade and the rising river, the price of wool and the corruption of the New York State Legislature. The conversation paused during a rumble of thunder. Shorty raised his right eyebrow and glanced at his son who was on his feet and headed toward the window. The sky outside had darkened as a bank of black clouds moved in. Rain spattered against the window. "Pa, we better get a move on," the young giant said in quiet urgent tones as he stooped to look out the window toward the sky.

A crack of thunder interrupted them and almost instantly the room was illuminated by a bolt of lightning.

Little dove under the table, yelled "Incoming, incoming" and held his head in his hands, shaking.

Shorty backed away from the window and in a low tone said, "Lightnin'. Close one."

Yukon was up on his toes, back arched, neck bristling. Then he slunk under the table close to Jo Mary and whimpered. Jo Mary glanced under the table in surprise and said, "Easy does it, guys. We're all safe, no one hurt."

"Close one," Shorty whispered, "This ain't Afghanistan. You're home safe, Son." Then to Jo Mary, "That coyote dog of yours is drawing it down on us. Ain't he got no place of his own?"

"He sleeps with me. This is his place." Jo Mary replied calmly.

Little pulled his great hulk out from under the table, rose up to his full height, took several deep breaths, shook his head fiercely and let out an ear-shattering, "Wa-woo-woohoo, wa-woo woohoo.! And he said, "That took me back. I was right there, right on top of one of those ridges. You can never get it out of you."

Shorty reached to put an arm around his shoulder, "You home now," he said.

An avalanche of hail and rain poured down on the cabin roof. Wind gusts swayed the pines visible through the windows. Jo Mary said, "Good thing you boys hung around for dinner. You might not have made it back to the Post in this. Guess I'll have to put up with your company for the night."

Shorty said, "Lucky we're snug in this hacienda of yours, Missy. " My boy is a little shaky about lightnin' since he got back from the Middle East."

"We can't stay here, Pa," said Little, "it'll pass."

"Sure we can stay," Shorty objected. "Lightnin' storms are bad medicine. The river'll be runnin' rough, too."

"I got plenty of room, your father can have the extra downstairs bedroom and you can have the loft. No problem. I insist. You've got to stay."

So it was settled. The storm continued, Jo Mary popped some corn, and poured another round of Southern Comfort. Shorty John produced a pipe and smoked comfortably as they talked of old times. Jo Mary told the story of Grampa Tinker killing the eight-hundred pound black bear whose hide now made a bed for Yukon.

Finally Shorty said, "I know you don't want to talk about it but Sasquatch and Injuns go a long way back, Mohawk people call them Stone Giants. Their skin so tough you couldn't hurt 'em with a arrow. They came into our territory and near drove us out. They was cannibals. We caught 'em, not me, this was long time ago, our people caught 'em in a narrow canyon and we buried them with rocks, some got away so we see 'em now and again. Don't talk much about 'em, scares people too bad think about they eat people.

Lot of stories the old guys tell 'bout them. Big tall, taller than Little here." He winked at his son, "course Little is better lookin'."

Before his father could get any further into the subject, Little stood up to his full six-foot-seven, took a mighty stretch and said, "If we are staying, Pa, it's time for bed. Lady don't want to hear any more of your scary stories tonight and I don't either. You're giving me the creeps. It's spooky enough around here without you make it worse."

Jo Mary yawned and stretched, too. "He's right, Shorty. It's gettin' late. We'll talk tomorrow." She got up and motioned Little towards the loft. "Bed's all made up. There are extra blankets in the bureau drawers if you need 'em."

She approached Shorty, "Come on, get up, you get the presidential suite."

Shorty grumbled but pushed himself forward on the couch and rose up unsteadily. Jo Mary walked to the bedroom door off the dining room and opened it for him. "There's a thunder mug under the bed in case you need it." Shorty limped past her and smiled and nodded her a good night.

Jo Mary retired to the master bedroom off the living room. Yukon followed in close behind and seemed especially pleased to leap up onto the soft woolen blankets and lay at Jo Mary's feet. The Johns had been sociable house guests here before. With the exception of the Sasquatch discussion, tonight's dinner with them had been pleasant. She went to sleep to the rhythmic drumming of rain on the roof, thinking about the old days when the big family gathered around the oak table and Grandma had to have Grampa put three leaves into it to make it big enough. That was when the two smaller cabins were still useable and there was room for lots of Tinkers on the place. She whispered to herself and Yukon, "We should have more company."

Jo Mary had been sound asleep dreaming about riding wild horses. She kept being thrown off and then bouncing back into the saddle like a rubber doll. There was no way she could stay on until she grabbed the horse's mane and bit its ear. Then the horse screamed and she awoke to hear screaming. The digital clock on her dresser flashed into view. It was 2:30 a.m. She sat bolt upright.

Yukon's head and ears jerked up but he made no move to leave the bed.

The screams turned into Shorty John's shouts and the thumping of him moving around in his room noisily. "Geronimo, Geronimo, I seen it. I seen that Stone Giant. He was right there in the window. Lightnin' lit him up like Broadway. Big red face, black hair down to his eyebrows, grinning at me with them big teeth. I see him right out there."

Jo Mary, heart pounding, pulled a knitted afghan over her flannel nightgown and ran into the living room. By the dim yellow glow of a battery-operated night light she saw Shorty burst from his room. A terrifying sight in long underwear, his long gray hair flying about as he waved a flashing ten-inch Bowie knife and danced about dragging his bad leg. "Where my big gun at?" he demanded. "Little, what you done with the 50 caliber? Quick get me a gun."

Little, with his pony tail unbound and dressed only in boxers and a plaid shirt, came down the stairs in two long strides and a leap that landed him next to his father. He saw the flash of the knife and flicked the blade out of the old man's hand sending it clattering across the floor. "Don't wave that thing around. Someone get cut bad." He shouted, "What happened? What'd you see?

"Stone Giant outside, where's the gun?"

Jo Mary had found a plastic flashlight in a side cabinet. She shouted calmly, "No guns. I told you, no shootin' around my place."

Little had his father in a bear hug with the old man's feet a few inches off the floor. Shorty was struggling to get free but did not stand a chance in his giant son's powerful grip.

"Set me down you pup, set me down."

"OK, OK, but you calm down." Both men were out of breath as Little sat his father back on the couch and stood up to catch his own wind. "You'll give yourself a heart attack you keep up like that, just like Uncle Two Elk John done. Doc up Ogdensburg told you 'Don't get excited.'"

"What's that old quack know? They was some kind of thing, I'm telling you, a Sasquatch or Stone Giant outside that window."

Jo Mary said, "Let's get some lights on. Little, go out in the kitchen and throw the generator switch; it's that red one by the door to the shed. Then we can put on the outside floodlights and see what's what." In a minute the hum of the propane generator could be heard and the indoor lights came on.

In that minute, Jo Mary had gone to the gun rack over the door and taken down her 38 Winchester. She kept it carefully pointed at the floor. Little said, "How about the big gun?"

Jo Mary said, "No big guns. I don't trust you two with a big gun."

Shorty John, having caught his breath, muttered, "I don't trust you with that pea shooter. Keep it pointed down."

Jo Mary said "OK. I got this just in case there is somethin' out there."

"In case? I just told you what's out there!" The old man yelled.

She went to the floodlight switch beside the front door, flicked it on and the yard all around the cabin was flooded with light. The three of them worked their way out the front door and into the light rain on the front porch.

Yukon edged cautiously in front of Jo Mary. He froze and turned his head toward the corner of the house that led to the window of the bedroom which Shorty had occupied. Yukon let out a low growl and then barked looking at Jo Mary in a worried eager way. All eyes were on the dog. As the party edged toward that end of the porch, Jo Mary pumped a shell into the chamber of her rifle.

She was the first to reach the corner of the house and peer around into the brightly lit side yard. The whiteness of a splintered pine next to the cabin struck her eye. The tree had been decapitated; its trunk split down to the earth. Her eyes flicked to rain dripping from the eves and to the puddles beneath them. There, lying flat on his back, stretched out in shallow water was the great mass of a Sasquatch, orange-faced and black-haired just as Jo Mary had depicted him in her painting. In his right hand he clutched a handful of Trillium blossoms. Jo Mary sobbed.

Chapter 7

Jo Mary halted as the scene burned into her brain. Droplets of falling rain glistened in the brilliance of the floodlight. The body of the Sasquatch looked monstrous so brightly lit against the surrounding blackness and all was pervaded by the stench of singed hair and flesh.

Little came slowly around the corner after Jo Mary. He hesitated only a second, then lunged forward to kneel by the side of the Sasquatch. He raised his own massive fist and delivered a thunderous punch to the center of its great chest.

"What are you doin'?" Jo Mary shouted tearfully as she jerked forward. "He's dead!"

Demunitive Shorty John was alongside her in an instant, crouching, staring intently. "Maybe he's not dead, better shoot. Stinks." He reached for the rifle that Jo Mary couched in the angle of her arm.

She yanked away, pointing the gun first at Shorty, then at Little who had two fingers pressed to the right side of the Sasquatch's throat. Shorty disappeared back around the corner of the cabin as the gun swept past him. "Get away" she yelled at the giant younger man.

Little raised a hand with his palm faced towards Jo Mary, the fingers of his other hand still on the Sasquatch's throat. "No pulse," he said, then in explanation, "Lightening, cardiac arrest."

Jo Mary dimly comprehended that Little might be trying to save the life of this creature that she had tried to befriend. She turned the rifle away.

"Better punch again," Little said, looking questioningly at Jo Mary. She nodded and the great fist delivered another blow. "You know CPR?" he grunted at her as he put his hands over the Sasquatch's heart, leaned forward and began delivering rhythmic compressions.

Jo Mary nodded again, laid her rifle down cautiously, and got on her knees alongside the out-sized head. She took a deep breath, placed her lips on the great red lips of the Sasquatch and blew the breath of life into him. Jo Mary and Little continued their lifesaving efforts for about three minutes when Shorty John came back holding his nose with one hand and his Bowie knife in the other.

"Why you still fight him?" he said, with a puzzled look. "He done for."

Little quickly felt for a carotid pulse again. "Pa, he's not dead. I got a pulse now. Keep blowing, Jo Mary."

Shorty addressed them pleading, "Get off him. I pay you plenty money for that hide. Don't mess him up." Shorty grabbed his son's shoulder trying to pull him away.

Little shrugged his father's hold off his shoulder and went on with cardiac compression. The Sasquatch shuddered and took a breath. Jo Mary lifted her head, looked at Little and exclaimed, "He's breathin'."

The Sasquatch coughed and sputtered.

Little stopped the tiring work of compressing the massive chest and placed a hand on Sasquatch's rising and falling abdomen. He checked the pulse once more and, nodding his head smiled, "Full and regular."

Shorty bent over them, his eyes dancing with angry excitement. "No good, no good," he said. "Stone Giant bad medicine, bring more Stone Giants make trouble for Injun people. I slit his throat," he gasped, brandishing the Bowie knife.

Little kept his own bulk between his father and the Sasquatch as he rolled the beast onto its right side and held its chin up to keep his airway open. The Sasquatch coughed and brought up blood-streaked gobs, then lapsed into snoring as he lay limply on his side.

Looking intently at the giant Indian, Jo Mary said, "You're right. Lightnin' must have stopped his heart. Is he OK?"

Little nodded, "Back in Afghanistan, I saw it. Spent too much time up at Firebase Phoenix. Those mountains around Korangel were bad for lightning, especially if you're big. If you punched them quick, some guys come out OK."

"He's gonna' make trouble," Shorty interrupted. "Better you let him choke. We could skin 'em, and stuff 'em. Tourists would pay good for a look-see."

"Shorty, you're crazy, he's almost human. You can't kill him," Jo Mary insisted, crowding the little man and his knife away.

"Pa, he's her pet. He's been bringing her flowers," Little said, handing his father one of the Trillium blossoms the Sasquatch had held in his hand. "Besides, this may be a scientific discovery. Think of the headlines, 'Mohawk tribal museum discovers the Missing Link.' Be good for business."

Yukon had remained at a judicious distance back on the porch but now he hopped down and moved slowly into the scene. He approached the unconscious, heavy-breathing Sasquatch, sniffing and growling tentatively. When he got no response, he bared his teeth and barked in the Sasquatch's face.

"Yukon! Down!" Jo Mary ordered, pointing sharply at the ground. She repeated the command. Yukon lowered himself reluctantly and moved away. She went to him, scratched him behind the ears and whispered, "Good dog, Good dog Yukon. This guy may get to be a friend of ours."

"That dog knows," Shorty shook his head in disagreement with Jo Mary. Then, changing his tone, he looked at his son and said, "You think the Albany paper, travel section, pick this up?"

"Yes Pa, for sure."

The Sasquatch stayed in what seemed like a heavy sleep. The three rescuers conferred, then rolled him onto a blanket and, with much sliding, tugging and hoisting, contrived to get him into the cabin and onto the couch in front of the fireplace. Shorty argued for tying his hands behind his back and lashing him to the couch.

Little talked him out of that, reminding his father, "Remember how you went nuts when you woke up in restraints the time you were in the hospital and they took your gall bladder, over to Watertown?" Shorty scratched his chin and went to stoke up the fire. Jo Mary pulled out a pillow and some wool blankets from a chest in Shorty's room and they tucked the Sasquatch in like a babe.

Little hovered close by the Sasquatch. He said, "When this fella comes to he's going to be weak and all mixed up. Won't know what hit him. Probably never been close to people. He's going to be scared."

Jo Mary said, "So what do we do?"

Shorty said, "If he goes nuts on us, back to plan 'A', I shoot 'em."

"Pa, we have got to be cool. Treat him like one of the family who has been sick. That's all we got to do. Just make nice."

Jo Mary said, "What if thinks we did this to him? I have got a confession to make. I took a shot at him this afternoon to scare him away from the cabin."

"So who's to blame him if he's suspicious of us?" Little said.

He stood up tall, walked to the front door, pulled it open and said, "We leave this wide open and stay out of his way. He'll hurt all over and be weak as a kitten. Maybe just like to stay warm. We'll stay quiet and let him make the first move."

Shorty said, "Jo Mary, you keep that gun on him."

"We don't know how he's going to act but we got to protect ourselves. I know you're good with that gun but I don't know if you ever killed anyone close up. I'll take care of that end if you want," Little offered.

Jo Mary took the rifle down and said, "Thanks, I got it covered."

Little said, "Ok. We had a few guys knocked out by lightning up on those mountain ridges in Afghanistan. If they came out of it they were pretty woozy."

"You were in Afghanistan?" Jo Mary said.

Little snapped to attention, saluted smartly and said, "Second Battalion 503rd regiment… Air Born, Ma'm."

"Everybody round here thought you were in jail for stealin' that old truck and wreckin it."

"I was drunk; judge gave me a choice so I joined up."

"Well thank the Lord; somethin' good come of it."

Things were quiet for a few minutes. All eyes were on the sleeping Sasquatch. His oversized body diminished the apparent size of the couch. Jo Mary had Little go into the kitchen, make a pot of coffee for them and warm a pan of milk for Sasqui. He poured coffee for all of them and sat the milk pan down on the floor beside the Sasquatch.

"Poor guy, first we flooded him out of his cave, then we shoot at him and now he's struck by lightnin'."

Shorty said, "He scared the livin' daylights out of me. Got no business peepin' in a window at a person like he done."

Jo Mary said, "Little, you saved Sasqui's life."

"You got a name for him? You call him Sasqui?" Little asked.

"Yes, Sasqui, that's the way I been callin' him to myself. I thought you wanted him dead."

Little, standing upright looming over the scene with a steaming mug in his hand grinned, "I did want him dead. Wanted to help Pa put him up for winter meat. But I got looking at this guy and thinking, 'Maybe us big guys should stick together.' And I saw this lightening thing a few times over there in the war. Just reflex I guess."

The Sasquatch groaned and swung a great arm around across his forehead as if to comfort a throbbing head.

Little said, "Sasqui huh, OK let's call him that now and just stay calm. Make him feel at home. Come to think of it, he looks a lot like Uncle Two Bears. You think so, Pa?"

Shorty gave the Sasquatch another look and mumbled, "Maybe." Then he went on, "You learn this in the Army? I told you to, 'Join the Air Force.' This Stone Giant, bad business."

"Shh, Pa, call him Sasqui. He'll put the Trading Post on the map. Folks will come from all over to see the Croghan Stone Giant or even if he's a Sasquatch."

The Sasquatch moaned and threw his other arm up over the first, embracing his head. He opened his mouth and licked his lips. Blood dripped onto his ruddy chin from the bite wound in his tongue. He opened his right eye and then his left, apparently not understanding what he saw.

He threw his great hairy legs around onto the floor and sat slouching upright with his head in his hands. Bent forward this way a raw patch of burned skin became apparent on his right shoulder. A racking cough took him and he brought up another bloody slug that he spat out onto Jo Mary's beautiful Hudson Bay blanket. A deep sigh followed the cough as he filled his cleared lungs with fresh warm air.

The three rescuers sat quietly in their chairs facing Sasqui from the right side of the fireplace and leaving him a clear path to the open door. Jo Mary sat with her rifle on the floor close at hand, the Johns sat quietly alert. Yukon's head was up, ears erect, body still.

Chapter 8

The living room of the cabin was now dimly lit by a single electric bulb shielded with a metal shade and suspended over the couch on which the Sasquatch reclined. The first bit of morning light was breaking through the porch window and the open front door.

The Sasquatch's gaze was captured by Yukon's twitching ears. When Yukon remained otherwise immobile, the Sasquatch slowly turned his hairy watermelon-sized head from right to left surveying the room, its contents and its other occupants. Shorty, Little and Jo Mary moved not a muscle. His eyes came to rest on Jo Mary and the Trillium blossom Little had retrieved from the scene of his accident. After a moment his broad Sasquatch face broke into what Jo Mary took for a gigantic smile.

Jo Mary smiled back.

"Welcome Sasqui," she whispered and pointed to the pan of milk.

Sasqui eyed the milk and eyed the two Indians and the dog. The Indians remained very still with smiles frozen. Sasqui reached down for the pan with both hands and lifted it to his mouth. He sipped, at first keeping an eye on the others and then concentrated on a long, long thirsty drink, licked his lips and set the empty pan down on the floor.

After he had wiped his mouth with his arm, Jo Mary said softly, "Well sir, you're welcome."

A querulous look came over his expressive face. He lurched forward and suddenly vomited the milk which was now stained pink with blood. He wretched and wretched till Jo Mary came to the couch beside him and took his great head between her hands, one arm on his forehead, the other behind his head. With his head supported this way, Sasqui went on retching several more times and then rolled back into the couch, gently freeing his head with a sigh.

"Just a big baby," Shorty chuckled.

"I told you he'd be sick," Little shrugged. Both of them remained warily seated.

Jo Mary stayed on the couch not far from Sasqui but no longer touching him. Sasqui, beside her, rocked his head slowly from side to side and looked miserable. Gradually the movements slowed, his breathing grew deeper, and his head fell back against the couch and then slid, coming to rest on top of Jo Mary.

She braced herself against the great weight of his head and shoulders. In the midst of her struggle to support him she became aware of his pungent aroma: burnt hair, burnt flesh, vomit and great hairy unwashed body. Catching her breath she whispered, "Shh, he's asleep."

Sasqui stayed asleep as they pried Jo Mary out from under him and stuffed blankets and pillows in her place. With more bedding and incorporating the couch, they formed a kind of a nest for him there in the living room. Little got a mop and bucket from the shed and cleaned up where Sasqui had vomited and bled. Shorty kept Yukon from licking up the vomit. "You dumb dog, you want to catch leprosy? Get out of there," he said, roughly herding the dog out of the way.

Jo Mary dressed the wound on Sasqui's shoulder with Neosporin ointment and gauze pads from the first aid cabinet. Her mind worked rapidly. "I have to keep these John boys here until I figure a way to keep them from goin' back to the Trading Post and tellin' stories. I've got me a live Sasquatch on this island and I think maybe the two of us could get along. How do I keep the John boys or their customers from killin' him or him from killin' them? Shorty wants to skin him and stuff him to show off at the Post. Little seems to want to keep him alive and make a sideshow freak out of him. And Lord knows what Sasqui's got on his own mind. What in the hell does he want? Does he have a mind?

Little must have been chewing the situation over, too, because that afternoon, after the place was cleaned up, Sasqui made comfortable and they had eaten baloney sandwiches and coffee for lunch, Little said, "Jo Mary, we got to talk."

Jo Mary nodded warily, "Oh, yeah, what about?"

"About him," he answered raising his eyebrows and nodding toward the Sasqui.

Jo Mary glanced at the sleeping giant and back at the Indians, then agreed with a thoughtful nod of her own.

Little said, "Pa, you want in on this?"

"You bet I do. Let's get out on the porch away from this stink and where what's-his-name, the lunk head there," indicating, the Sasqui, "won't hear us."

"Don't be callin' the poor fella names. He may take offense," Little said, motioning towards the door. "Come on out on the porch."

Jo Mary said, "Grab some cushions out of the chest by the door. Chairs are wet out there."

The three filed out onto the cabin porch, each with an arm load of cushions with which they lined the wooden Adirondack chairs that Grampa Tinker had built during an idle winter, years before. The rain stopped but dark clouds lowered over the island. The clouds reflected Jo Mary's unhappy speculation about what Shorty and Little had in mind for Sasqui.

Why can't they just go home and leave us be? she thought. Poor Sasqui, he has been livin' on his own out in this beautiful country. Now civilization has caught him in the teeth of its damn gears and wants to grind him into a plastic toy for idiots to gape at. He should live wild and free or however in hell he wants to live.

She saw the parallel with her own life. That's pretty much what I got. I like it out here alone   and I been here most all my life. Why should we have to put up with this "bullshit," she exclaimed out loud.

The two Indians, unaccustomed to profanity, sat in rigid silence.

Jo Mary shook her head, "Sorry, I'm just going in circles here, things are happenin' too fast for me. If I cuss a little it helps bump me off the merry-go-round. Know what a mean?"

"White folks cuss. Injuns don't. I don't know how come we don't. Just don't," Shorty said in a conciliatory tone. Little nodded without comment.

"OK Little, you called this pow wow, what's on your mind?" Jo Mary said.

He took a deep breath and said, "That Sasquatch, he could be worth a heap of money but he's a big animal, could easy hurt someone if he gets riled. And he's sick. Maybe needs a vet."

Shorty said," We all three got a financial interest here. Maybe I put a rope around him, break him like a horse. If he need a vet, we'll pay for him, to protect our interest."

Jo Mary brightened. She thought she saw a way out. "You're right boys; we all worked to save Sasqui's life. I suppose in some kind 'a way we all do own a interest in him. How 'bout if I buy you two out at say a hundred dollars apiece, cash money right here and now."

Shorty snorted, "Missy, a hundred dollar, a hundred dollar, no way, no can do, I put him in a cage in backroom at the Tradin' Post, charge five dollar a look-see. Maybe go on tour with circus. Maybe do big time Vegas show; he's worth a hundred grand easy."

Jo Mary bristled. "This is my place, my property. If anybody owns that critter, I do. Thanks for your help, boys, but this palaver is gettin' kind of tiresome."

Little leaned forward with a hand raised, palm forward in a gesture of peace. "Jo Mary, Pa, ease off, ease off. We're getting ahead of ourselves here. How do we get this critter well and keep him from eating one of us? That's what we should be talking about right now."

When they came out on the porch Jo Mary had carefully closed but not latched the door so their talk and the snap of the latch would not disturb the sleeping Sasqui. Now, glancing past Little, she detected a bit of movement of the door. She pointed silently with her right index finger and all three fixed their eyes on the door as it very slowly opened. In the interior darkness they could make out the dark mass of Sasqui standing erect, his eyes reflecting the dull exterior light. Standing familiarly beside him was Yukon with his tail erect and wagging slowly.

Yukon was the first to move after the door opened. He trotted out onto the porch and over to Jo Mary, nuzzling her leg for a scratch. Sasqui followed Yukon slowly, looked at the others sitting in a semicircle of chairs and sat himself down awkwardly in the one remaining chair. Once seated he leaned against the back of the chair, like the others, then squinted at Little who had crossed his long legs. Sasqui reached for his own foot and pulled his legs into a similar position. Shorty held his hands clasped with fingers entwined over his prominent belly. Sasqui observed Shorty's pose for a moment and adopted a similar posture.

Jo Mary watched this tableau develop with a quizzical look on her face as she scratched Yukon's ears and stroked his head. After Sasqui, like a visiting neighbor, had settled a moment, Yukon trotted over to him and his big hairy hand came down to stroke the coarse grey-brown fur along the dog's spine. Yukon spun around, confidently pursuing Sasqui's vomit-stained hand and after Sasqui had let him catch it licked the sour substance from its back.

Little, making as if he would rise, was the first to speak, "I'll get your Winchester, Jo Mary. Case you want it." This was more asking permission than a declaration of intent.

Jo Mary raised her hand to restrain him and said, "No, we don't need that. The damn thing would probably go off and put a slug through your foot."

The four, five if you include Yukon, sat for an hour in those rustic chairs on the cabin porch. Clouds gradually cleared, the sun broke through in places and began to dry the planks of the porch and the scrub surrounding it.

Sasqui turned out to be an almost perfect mime. He imitated facial expressions, postures and even, using his fingers alongside his head, did a likeness of Yukon paying attention with his ears. Shorty took out a plug of tobacco and bit off a chunk. Sasqui watched carefully and then held an imaginary plug of his own in his hand and pretended to bite off a chunk. He chewed vigorously then stuck his tongue into his cheek making it bulge as if he had a wad of tobacco parked there just as Shorty had.

Shorty chuckled, "He's got that down just right. I bet I could teach him Injun sign language."

Little said, "Maybe he can talk."

"I ain't heard him make a sound so far," Jo Mary said.

"Try to sign with him some, Pa."

Shorty moved around in his chair and squinted at Sasqui straight on. Then he opened his mouth and said slowly in a loud clear voice, "How you doin'?" He repeated this phrase and pointed to his lips as he spoke. Then he pressed the nail of his right index finger against his thumb and flicked it toward Sasqui.

Sasqui gave Shorty a look, straight back at him squint for squint, opened his mouth and coughed. Then he held his extended flat right hand, back upward, in front of his chest, moved it to the right turning, the thumb up and then brought it back to the original position. Next he made the same flicking sign with his right thumb and index finger that Shorty had made.

"I be a monkey's uncle," Shorty said and slapped his right hand to his forehead. "He can't talk. He say he can't talk and he says it real good in Injun sign."

Jo Mary exclaimed, "You mean he said somethin' to you with that finger wiggle-waggle? I don't believe it. Maybe it was coincidence or he was just imitatin' you."

Reacting to the activity Yukon got up from where he had positioned himself at the head of the porch steps and walked over to stand beside Jo Mary's chair and fix his gaze on Sasqui.

Little said, "Wave your hand like that, thumb up, that means no. Even I know that and I'm no good at sign. Pa has it down pat."

"He made the 'No' sign. I never showed it to him," Shorty said.

Sasqui sat back and seemed to ponder the amazement of his audience but volunteered no more coughs or signs. His great bushy brows gathered, creating a deep furrow between his eyes. He leaned forward with his chin on his right fist and elbow resting on his knee.

What is he thinkin'? Jo Mary wondered. He looks as if he's afraid, he's spilled the beans. Maybe that lightnin' mixed him up, knocked his guard down. He was always so shy and scary. Now he's bein' all palsey-walsey.

Yukon accepted a pat from Jo Mary and then walked over to Sasqui and cocked his head at him. Sasqui eyed him back, gave him a rough stroking. Then Yukon laid down beside his chair contentedly.

"Pa, see if he knows that bear story, that you got from watchin' them do it in sign on the internet."

"Internet just refresh my memory. That's Bitter Root Jim's story. Too long. I do it some other time, maybe."

"Ask him if he's hungry. Maybe his stomach has settled," Mary Jo suggested.

Then Shorty faced Sasqui directly again, sitting up very straight and looking him questioningly in the eye. He placed the little finger side of his right hand against his stomach and sawed back and forth.

Sasqui watched carefully and responded by raising his right hand with the index finger extended and moving the hand toward his chest as he folded his index finger over his thumb. He repeated the motion purposefully and then made Shorty's sawing motion across his stomach.

"He say, 'Yes, he very hungry.'"

Shorty and Sasqui faced each other with a serious quiet demeanor and made a series of signs back and forth as Jo Mary and Little sat back and watched.

"Can you understand what they are saying?" Jo Mary asked.

"My Indian signing's not so good anymore. I catch a couple things. Think he's telling Pa he didn't mean to scare him. I just caught the 'Thanks' sign from Sasqui. I think Pa's made a new friend."

"Isn't it amazin' Sasqui can talk in sign? He looks like an overgrown chimpanzee that had a bear for a grandfather but now that he's quieted down, he's charmin'."

"About 500 pounds of lean muscle "charming." He still got me a little nervous. But Pa's about ready to invite him to the Trading Post for a beer."

"How does he know the language? Is that Mohawk or English?"

"It ain't either one, it's just sign. Like nodding your head is yes and shaking it is no in any language. Old folks got these Stone Giant stories. They say way back there were a few that survived the big battle where most of them were buried in a ravine under rocks. Those few lived way back in the mountains, in caves mostly, but they come out sometimes and they do some tradin' with Injuns or steal stock. Different tribes have their own names for them, Big Foot, Hairy Monster, Ghost Ape. Pa calls them Stone Giants or Stone Warriors. I guess us Injuns was better organized than the Stone Giants. So after they got beat they kept by themselves, especially after we got guns. Maybe arrows wouldn't hurt them but guns were a whole 'nuther story. Old folks say they are out there keeping an eye on what's going down. I never put much store by any of it but now maybe I got another think coming."

Jo Mary nodded her head. "No one would believe me when I told about seein' 'em on our place. Thought I was loony. But I knew what I saw. There was a whole family of them used to sleep in a cave under those bluffs." Jo Mary pointed to the cliff where she had watched Sasqui recently. When I was a kid, I always thought they had a better deal than me, out in the woods all the time, didn't have to go to school, and could go swimmin' whenever they felt like it, kid stuff."

"Seeing is believing," Little shrugged. "This guy is real."

Shorty broke away from Sasqui, placing a hand on his arm as if to say, Hold on a minute. He turned to Jo Mary and his son, "This is a pretty smart Sasquatch. Can sign better than me. I told him about how he got knocked over by lightnin' and how my boy here worked his medicine magic and brought him back to life. He gets it, an' he's real grateful for us bringin' him back, an' he says thanks, specially to you, Jo Mary, for all the food you left around for him and for that poultice you put onto his sore shoulder."

"Well, tell him he's welcome and we are so sorry the damn federal government flooded out his house down in the caves," Jo Mary said. She reached over to emphasize welcome with the intention of shaking hands but when she saw that great ham of a hand she thought better of it, just smiled and tapped the back of it.

Shorty said, "Let's don't get off on the wrong foot about the federal government wreckin' his home. I want to do some business with him so I don't want him thinkin' any friends of ours are responsible for the mess he is in. I'll just tell him he's welcome and we all glad to help out." Shorty made a few signs and

Sasqui smiled and nodded, gently touching the back of Jo Mary's hand.

Jo Mary's eyes teared up and her voice quivered. Finally she got out, "Sasqui, we'll have you better soon and you can get back in the woods somewhere and live in peace again. I know you must hate all these goings-on and people and guns and store-bought food and all, must make you as sick as it does me. Sicker, cause you're used to having the woods all to your lonesome. Don't you worry; we'll get you back there."

Sasqui seemed to react to the emotion of her speech, whether or not he understood the words. For a moment, he seemed about to take her into his huge arms. The two Indians braced and exchanged glances of concern. Sasqui reacted as if he sensed their alarm and instead of a hug he smiled, leaned his head to one side and nodded his head gently in the "yes" sign.

Little said, "I guess you two understand each other. Now how's chances of some pancakes. It's getting past my breakfast time."

Jo Mary blew her nose in a big blue paisley kerchief she pulled out of the back pocket of her jeans. "Sure thing, Shorty. Comin' right up."

"You go help Jo May," Shorty said to his son, "I want to tell Sasqui about Injun show business and how him and me could stake us to a heap of cash if we play this right."

"You sure you're OK out here alone with the big guy?" Little whispered in his father's ear.

"Hey, no problem, Sasqui an' me, gonna be buddies," he said, reaching up to pat the towering Sasqui on his good shoulder. "We speak the same language."

Jo Mary and Little retreated into the cabin, leaving the other two huddled with hands and arms moving rapidly in an intense conversation.

Chapter 9

It was noon by the time the four were gathered around the dining room table finishing up the huge platter of corn pancakes and bacon that Jo Mary had prepared. Sasqui worked hard at imitating the use of forks and knives by the others. In the end, he ate mostly with his hands lifting one or two dinner-plate sized pancakes toward his mouth and nibbling at them. The bacon did not appeal to him at all but he lapped up maple syrup with great interest. He was able to hold down a quart of milk sipping it slowly.

Yukon came to the table staring at Jo Mary, obviously hoping for a handout but she stuck to the rule of no table food for dogs. Shorty and Little abided by the rule as well, despite Yukon's artful begging. But when Yukon approached Sasqui, he was met with a big smile and a handful of bacon which Yukon grabbed quickly and ran to a corner of the hearth to gobble down.

Jo Mary laughed but shook her head in the universal "No, No" sign. The Indians laughed, too, and Sasqui did not offer Yukon second helpings.

After all the food on the table had been eaten, they lingered over mugs of coffee. Sasqui had mastered the coffee mug but only after careful intervention to make him aware of how hot the coffee was. The old-fashioned hotel-style mug looked like a child's tea cup in his over-sized hands and Jo Mary had to stifle a laugh when she saw him raise a pinky as he sipped.

Sasqui caught her mirth and played up the maneuver. Shorty and Little caught on and lifted pinkies as well as they sipped. Jo Mary joined in, leading to much hilarity.

Jo Mary was the first to recover. She said, "He's a regular clown."

"He's a kidder," Little laughed.

Then Jo Mary looked serious, "How are we goin' to get this poor guy back into some mountains where he can live like a proper Sasquatch? Civilization is ruinin' him."

Shorty said, "Hold on there. Hold your horses, Missy. Who says Stone Giants want to live in mountains?"

"Well a' course they do. You ever see any Sasquatch in town?"

"I seen this one on my ranch. Tryin' to steal a heifer."

"How you know it was Sasqui, Mary Jo countered?"

"I recognize him alright… an' he just told' me he was sorry he knocked me down the way he done."

"He told you that?

"On the porch, while you was cookin'."

Shorty turned to Sasqui who sat to his left occupying almost a third of the big oak table's circumference. Making a few signs, Shorty filled him in on what he had just told Jo Mary.

Sasqui moved his head and shoulders from side to side, smiled sheepishly and rolled his eyes.

Jo Mary remembered old movie clips on TV of Lew Lehr doing his, "Monkey's is the kwaziest people" shtick. She thought Sasqui could pass for a very big man in a gorilla suit.

Shorty went on, "Stone Giant just like us, like prime beef, warm place for sleepin' in winter, maybe a Cadillac car, just like you and me. Only reason they ain't in town is, they scared of getting' shot."

"He told you that, too, I suppose," Jo Mary said, raising an eyebrow.

"Look at him," Shorty gestured toward the lounging Sasqui. "He's snugger than a bug in a rug here, out of the rain, maple syrup on his pancakes. Sure beats roots and rabbits. I can tell you that from eatin' plenty roots and rabbits."

Little looked at Sasqui who was scratching Yukon's ears after the dog had set his chin on the creature's hairy leg. Little nodded, "You're right there, Pa, he looks like a happy man, indoors here."

"Sasqui could never live in a city. They'd pass some damn law and put him into a zoo," Jo Mary insisted.

"Maybe, maybe not," said Shorty. "If he had a job and if people weren't scared of him, he might get along."

"Why would anyone be afraid of Sasqui? Look at him and Yukon there. He's just an old sweetheart," Jo Mary said.

Shorty looked uncomfortable. "Need to stretch my legs, Missy. Maybe me an' Sasqui have a walk, smoke a little tobacco together." With that he stood up and pulled a box of small cigars from the inside pocket of his beaded leather vest, held them up toward Sasqui and motioned to the door.

Little waited till they were outdoors and then seemed to reach a decision. He spoke directly to Jo Mary, "You know Pa insisted on coming over here because he was afraid that Stone Giant would hurt you. It wasn't a hunting expedition. It was to look out for you."

Jo Mary said, "Hogwash, I've been huntin' since I was six years old, I'm better armed out here than an airborne division and I can damned well take care of myself."

"I tried to talk him out of it... till he told me..."

Jo Mary stood up angrily, carrying a platter toward the kitchen. "Told you what?"

Little didn't answer. He started stacking plates where he sat. They cleared the table. He scraped the plates into a compost barrel outside the back door. She began washing the dishes in the galvanized iron sink. He stood towering alongside her and dried them.

Jo Mary broke the silence, "Now your old man's got that "dangerous" critter out front trying' to kill him with cee-gar cancer."

"I never smoked much till Afghanistan. Gets cold, lonesome in them mountains. Couple of smokes make you feel easy." Then out of the blue he said, "You ever wonder about why you got black hair and your family were all red heads?"

"What's it to you?" she said.

"It's something.'"

"I got no idea what's goin' on in your crazy Injun heads. First you come traipsin' here with your big guns when I told you to stay off my property. Then you come in here and take over the place, near killed the only survivin' Sasquatch in North America and now you're makin' insinuations about my god damn hair. "

"Easy, Jo Mary. Didn't mean to offend you. Just trying to explain to you what Pa told me."

"What, what did that nosey lyin' outlaw Injun tell you?" She wrung out the dishcloth like it was the neck of a chicken she was killing. Then she made a sudden move to hang it on a rack in front of which Little stood. "Get out of my way. Get out of my kitchen. You take up too God damn much space."

He moved out of the way slowly. "How is it that you never had red hair? I remember when your hair was jet black, straight as an arrow and longer than mine." He flipped his long, black ponytail at her with a sharp twist of his head.

She turned to him with a snarling lip," What the hell you mean? You makin' me some kind of Injun?"

He raised his voice, too, "Guess you got some blood in you. You look like you are about set to take scalps."

"I threatened to get the law on your pa and you and I'll do it."

"Calm yourself, Sister."

"Don't you "Sister" me none. What you gettin' at?"

"Come on in here and sit down," he said as he left the kitchen and sat down at the dining room table.

Jo Mary took three deep breaths and came to sit opposite Little. The sun had settled onto a low angle and cast long shadows against the cabin as it illuminated the interior with afternoon orange. Cigar smoke, still pleasant in its freshness, scented the air. Through the front window Sasqui and Shorty could be seen blowing smoke rings.

Little gazed steadily at Jo Mary and started in, "My pa and your ma grew up neighbors. Your ma was here on the Tinker place and Pa was on the farm in Croghan. They went to school together, saw each other at dances and had beers at the Black River Inn, that roadhouse used to be on the Nosenchuck Road."

"You're lyin'." Jo Mary exclaimed.

"That's the way Pa told me once when he had too much liquor in him. He said, 'We was just like that.'" Shorty held up his index and third finger crossed.

"But it was all on the sly. Their folks didn't neither side like it."

"He must 'a been drunk out of his mind."

"Then Pa went off to fight in Korea. He come home, thought there might be a chance for a Mohawk soldier and a red-headed Anglo girl. But by then your ma was married to a sandy-headed white guy and they had this little black-haired daughter named Jo Mary."

Jo Mary stood up frowning.

"That's why Pa thinks he's got to look out for you...Sis."

"Sis?" she echoed.

Chapter 10

Jo Mary was perplexed by Little's revelation that she was his sister, a daughter to Shorty and half Mohawk Indian. This has got to be some malarkey he dreamed up. But could it be? She stepped into the bedroom to look at herself in the bureau mirror. Folks used to say I looked a little "exotic." Am I white or Indian or what? Why didn't Ma tell me? Should I run these fakers off the place or should I sign up for a job dealing blackjack up at the Akwasasne casino. Who the hell am I?

Her brief reverie was interrupted by Shorty's yell from the porch "There's a moose out here," followed by, "Must be loco, tearin' up your garden."

Jo Mary and Little rushed out onto the porch where they could see a 3-or- 4-year-old bull moose snorting and pawing at what had been Jo Mary's kitchen garden. She had harvested the beans, corn and potatoes. All that remained were stalks and withered greens at which the big black beast tore furiously.

Jo Mary exclaimed , "Oh my God, first a Sasquatch and now a moose."

Shorty said, "He's a good lookin' animal. That rack on him is a keeper."

"Where you think he come from?" said Little.

"Maybe caught in the flood when they backed up the river. Probably scared of swimmin' in this fast water.

Little said, "He's got a couple of winters meat on him."

Shorty looked at Jo Mary with raised eyebrows, "If Missy here don't mind just a little shootin' "

She shook her head. " I told you guys I don't want you over here huntin'. Looks like he's on my property eaten' my garden so he belongs to me. I'll harvest him when I need the meat."

"That's a whole lot of moose. You sure you want to kill, butcher , store and eat all 1500 pounds on you own?" questioned Little. "We could help you with him and share up."

"This is not a huntin' preserve for you or those flat land tourists you bring around. Just leave that animal be."

The moose continued his destructive stamping and pawing in the garden.

Yukon stalked out toward the fearsome animal who then paused and stared at him and the gathering on the porch. Sasqui eyed the scene thoughtfully as he stubbed-out his cigar on the railing following Shorty's example.

"What are you goin' to do with him?" Shorty asked.

"He's just a big cow. I'll shoo him up to the pond on the north end of the property. When he gets wind of those juicy cattails up there he'll go." And saying this she stepped off the porch and walked toward the now silent staring moose.

"Shoo bossie," she said waving both arms in the direction of the pasture.

The moose stood his ground, lowered his head brandishing his very formidable antlers. He pawed a warning. Still, Jo Mary stepped forward confidently, "Shoo bossie."

Shorty said, "Missy, stand still. He's goin' to charge."

The bull snorted and pawed. Jo Mary suddenly realized she was in over her head and she froze in place.

Sasqui let out a squeal, put one hand on the porch rail, leaped over and ran toward the moose. The moose instantly shifted focus and fixed on Sasqui who was now rushing back and forth a few yards in front of the huge black creature. The bull lowered his head in Sasqui's direction and charged but Sasqui curved his run into a tight circle and the antlers missed.

Jo Mary took advantage of the distraction and ran back to the relative safety of the porch.

Now Sasqui was running, then walking, a slow pattern in front of the moose. The moose made some half-hearted charges and then settled to watch Sasqui's display. In a few moments the moose had calmed and Sasqui approached him with a handful of corn stalks.

"Son of a gun, will you look at that," whispered Shorty.

The moose grasped the stalks and chewed away at them vigorously.

Jo Mary said, "Shorty, will you tell Sasqui to take him away from the cabin up toward the pasture, please?"

"OK," Shorty said. He caught Sasqui's eye with a wave of his arm and made a few signs, then waved off toward the north. Sasqui nodded and soon was trotting off in that direction at the side of the great black creature. He looked back at the group on the porch and Shorty gave him the OK sign with a circle formed from the thumb and index finger. Sasqui smiled and returned the sign.

Shorty turned to Jo Mary, "Missy, you got to be careful round animal like that." He nodded his head wisely.

Jo Mary said, "Guess you're right there... Pa" and she grimaced.

He opened his mouth, leaned his head back and squinted and then responded,"Pa?"

Jo Mary let the question hang in the air. She returned to the cabin leaving the Johns on the porch where they conferred excitedly.

A half hour later when Sasqui was back, the group gathered in the living room in front of a TV screen. Little was saying to Jo Mary, "Looks like we found a job for Sasqui, we'll make him a rodeo clown. If he can do a moose like that, a bull would be a cinch for him." Jo Mary had reluctantly produced a CD of the 2012 Adirondack Championship Rodeo at Lake George's Painted Pony Ranch.

"Quit talkin' and get that disc goin'. I want to see what this big fella thinks of rodeo work," said Shorty.

"Be interestin' to see what he thinks of TV," Jo Mary added.

Little inserted the disc. On the screen a very large bull appeared jumping around with the agility of a poodle and the power of a spooked tiger as he tried to dislodge a cowboy on his back. The cowboy was holding on with one hand, waving a Stetson with the other and spending half of his time in the air.

Sasqui acted amazed. He felt the screen, looked behind the monitor, tapped it with his giant index finger and shook his head in perplexity. The others only glanced at the rodeo scene and then watched Sasqui. He looked from face to face of each of them, including Yukon, as if asking for an explanation. He settled on Shorty.

Shorty patted Sasqui on his wrist saying, "Shhh, shhh" and then made some quick signs that seemed to reassure him. The two sat back in the big mission chairs and fixed their attention on the rodeo.

It took a while for Sasqui to grasp the concept of TV. Shorty explained to the rest of them that at first Sasqui had thought there were small people and small animals trapped inside the box. But he had been able to persuade him that they were not real, that they were "like shadows of people and animals." They were shadows of real events that happened out there in the big world that Sasqui and his relatives had avoided for so long.

Sasqui shook his head in wonder and half belief as he watched the rodeo intently. He was particularly fascinated by the antics of the clowns and their ability to distract a stomping, snorting bull who was intent on trampling a cowboy he had just thrown. Sasqui approached the screen in those events and pointed approvingly at the clowns and then at himself.

Shorty elbowed his son who had taken a seat beside him, "Did yah see that, did ysh see that? He's got the idea."

Little responded nodding his head, "He was good with that moose. Maybe they were already pals."

Shorty sniffed, "He probably been makin' a livin' stealin' stock out towards Croghan. Probably ours before we had to shut down the farm."

Little said, " Lot more cows around than moose. Could be pay-back time, Pa."

Chapter 11

Jo Mary had been silent during the rodeo screening. Now she addressed the two Indians from her seat at the table where she had situated herself at a little distance from the others. She held up a hand, "Slow down there, guys. Sasqui here ain't ready for all that. He's got that burned shoulder, he just come-to after bein' hit by lightnin', DEC flooded him out of his house and up to now he has lived all his life hidin' out in the woods. You talk about your culture shock. This guy is like a space alien. He needs a chance to catch his breath."

Shorty looked back at her straight-in-the-eye, "You got any idea how many of my cows just wandered off over the years? You got any idea how hard it is makin' a livin' off tourists around here? He owes me, and besides we could show him a good time, maybe make him rich."

"She's got a point, Pa. This Sasqui here never mixed with people. First flu bug comes along is likely to kill him."

"If we don't get him to a doc or a vet or somebody that shoulder of his will get infected and that will kill him," Shorty countered.

Jo Mary said calmly, "I've taken care of worse scalds than that on horses. If it don't come around right away there ain't a vet in the lower 48 who wouldn't give his right arm to treat a Sasquatch. I'm worried about him personally and him as, let's face it, a rare biological specimen."

Shorty stood up angrily, "Specimen, specimen, we're talkin' dollars and cents here, money big money, money that's owed to me for those cows of mine he ate. If you got to bring him a vet out here who's going to pay for it? How you goin' to feed this bo hunk? He eats like a 500-pound gorilla. And you think he's always going to be so tame? What if he gets mad at you? You ever think of that?"

Little got up and stood between his father and Jo Mary. Sasqui and the dog shrunk away from the conflict. Little said, "Pa, don't get so excited. We can work this out." And then to Jo Mary, "Pa makes some sense. Are you really safe with this guy around? Can you take care of him?"

Jo Mary was on her feet as well now, face to chest with the towering Little. "Take care of him? He takes care of himself pretty good all these years and him and me been alone on this place ever since it turned into an island. He don't need no rodeo job. He don't need money, far as I can see. Him and me were doin' just fine until you two came along."

Little said, "Except this Sasqui here just got hit by lightning. I seen what that can do to folks. He's got that burn and I think the lightning did something to his brain, too. Something has changed him. Usually something is wrong when a wild animal acts friendly. You got no idea what's going to happen."

Shorty struggled to get around his son so he could confront Jo Mary. Jo Mary sputtered, "You don't know what you're talkin' about. Get, get off my land, get out of here," as she, too, tried to get at her opponent. But Little maneuvered to stay between the two.

Jo Mary stepped back toward the table where she picked up a china bowl full of leftover chili and hurled it at Shorty. The contents splattered across the room, dousing Little and hitting Shorty full in his ample belly. It fell to the floor and shattered. With arms flying all three scrambled to escape one another and the pungent sauce.

Their shouts and screams filled the cabin. Yukon leapt back into a corner out of the way. Little slipped in the mess on the floor and landed full-length flat on his back. Shorty, trying to escape, tripped over him, landing with both hands in the sauce. Jo Mary, scrambling backward, tripped on the bear skin rug.

Sasqui had begun to look uneasy as the tension built between Jo Mary and her other two guests. When Jo Mary had reached for the bowl and voices started to rise he had gotten to his feet and stepped toward the door. At the height of the fiasco he seemed to make up his mind. He took down the Remington 38 and broke it across his knee. Then with a roar none of them had ever heard before he grabbed the 50-caliber Sharps, swung it dangerously around his head and smashed it into the solid log frame of the front window. The window shattered and the rifle stock cracked so that it bent in two.

With his roar, all the other action in the cabin halted. Wild-eyed, Sasqui took one last look around the room and charged through the front door ripping it from its hinge. His three benefactors gradually got to their feet and peered out the front door in time to see him disappear toward the dock where the Zodiac and the John family's outboard were tied up.

Sasqui's demonstration instantly sobered the rest of them. Yukon went to licking up chili. Jo Mary fetched a wet towel from the kitchen and brought it to Shorty who was struggling to catch his breath.

She asked Little, "Are you all right? You didn't hit your head or anythin'?"

Little, wiping chili off his pigtail with both hands, said, "No, I think I'm OK. Better look at Pa."

She moved quickly back to Shorty, "I am so sorry; I lost my head for a minute." Tears ran down her cheeks and sobs stifled any further words.

Shorty was breathing easier. He laughed, "You got a temper on you. You're your mother's daughter all right." Dripping chili he got to his feet and leaned against Jo Mary.

Little interrupted, "So what about the big guy? I thought he was going to knock this place down. Look what he did to your rifles."

"He seemed so gentle before, but I am grateful that no one was between him and that door just now," Jo Mary said

"Talk about a temper, if he was to work for us as a rodeo clown we'd need another couple rodeo clowns to control him and maybe a stun gun," said Shorty.

Jo Mary became thoughtful, staring down the road after Sasqui. Then she said, "Where is he goin' to go to now? He's not a well animal and we just worked him into a fit. He could hurt himself."

She started out the door. Little grabbed her by one arm, "Without a gun? You saw what he could do, the way he smashed up that big Sharps of yours. Let him calm himself down before we go after him."

Jo Mary pulled away from Little. "I'm goin'. He could shoot himself or fall off that dock and get drowned."

The three of them walked down the road where they had last seen Sasqui. In some muddy patches along the way he had left his giant footprints. Little pointed to them, "Easy to see how they call him Big Foot.

Jo Mary said, "Don't see any blood so he's probably not cut."

They were almost in view of the shoreline when they heard a loud banging like an oil drum being beaten. They rushed to an elevated point on the road where the dock was in view. There was Sasqui in the John family's boat kicking holes in its bottom. He looked up from his rampage and saw them at the top of the hill. He let out another one of those horrendous roars, shook a warning fist at them, charged in their direction and retreated to the Zodiac. With his outlandish strength he pulled the bollards, with their mooring lines, free from the dock. The Zodiac drifted out into the Beaver River current, picked up speed and was swept toward the dam's spillway with its single passenger standing precariously erect at the boat's center.

Chapter 12

Jo Mary, Shorty and Little watched in amazement and then horror as they realized that their treasured find was heading for disaster. They rushed to the dock hoping that the other boat could somehow be made serviceable. The 17-foot fiberglass outboard had a two-foot-wide hole in its bow that Sasqui had punched or kicked in.

Shorty rubbed his chin thoughtfully as he stared at the wreckage. "That Stone Giant keeps costin' us more money. We should have shot him and stuffed him when we had the chance." He reached for a rifle that lay across a thwart, put it to his shoulder and sited toward the vanishing Zodiac.

Jo Mary was at the beached boat attempting to repair the hole by stuffing life jackets into it. She saw Shorty's move and yelled. "Shorty, don't."

Little yelled, "Pa, don't shoot," and he pushed Shorty's rifle barrel up in the air as it fired.

"You ruined that shot. I could have had him. He's gone crazy now. If he kills someone it's your fault," Shorty accused his son.

Little had the gun away from his father. He ejected a shell, detached the clip and stowed it in his pants pocket. "Never mind about that. Half hour ago he was our ticket to big time show business. You and Jo Mary brought it on with your fighting and yelling. Jo Mary, you should never a thrown that bowl of slops."

Jo Mary yelled back, "Help me with the boat. Maybe we can catch him before he goes over the spillway."

Shorty snorted, "Catch him? What you going to do when you catch him? He gone crazy, loco. Let him go over."

Little said, "Boat's no good. It'll float, but full of water, it won't make any time. He's too far ahead. Jo Mary, use the radio at the cabin. Maybe Sheriff Kelley can get to the dam before Sasqui and the Zodiac goes over the spillway."

Jo Mary was already jogging toward the cabin. Little shouted after her, "We'll see what we can do with the boat. Maybe we can get back to the truck and try to find him in case he got to shore."

In a few minutes, Jo Mary was back. The Johns had the boat alongside the dock. It floated six inches below its designed water line but the 90-horse Johnson was purring. She hopped in and Shorty steered the boat across current toward the old road. She spoke breathlessly, "Called Sheriff, told him, 'Sasquatch stole our Zodiac. Headed toward spillway. Be killed if he goes over.' He laughed. Said I been alone too long. I begged. Said he'd have the spillway checked. Look for a loose Zodiac… with a Big Foot steerin'. Big joke."

The trio piled into Shorty's Ford 350, Yukon enjoying an outdoor ride in the rear cargo area. The trio did a visual search of as much of the reservoir shore as they could see easily from the road which ran parallel to it. But they saw nothing.

The top two sections of the spillway closure had not yet been put in place. The flood of spring waters poured over its top like a virtual Niagara. The roar made them shout to hear one another. Sheriff Joe Kelley met them at the dam office. He shouted, "Joe Dingle… one of my deputies… found your Zodiac…on the south shore… half mile back…caught in a back eddy… snagged on a tree.

He ushered them into the office away from most of the roar. Kelley grinned as he shook hands with Shorty and Little, then offering a hand to Jo Mary, he said, "Got your boat for you. I was hoping to see a Sasquatch. Would have been my first one you know. But we would have gone after your boat even without that kind of embellishment," he laughed.

Jo Mary shook his hand silently, then stepped away for a long look out the office window at the forest, sky and water searching for a sign of her lost friend. The Sheriff took advantage of her momentary distraction. He glanced at the Johns and, with a big grin, shook his head, wound a finger around his right ear and pointed at Jo Mary.

Jo Mary, looking subdued, turned back to him saying, "Sheriff Kelley, I want to thank you kindly for all you did. I am much obliged to you. Hate to think of what replacin' that boat would cost me."

She turned to the Indians and winked. They nodded back at her, expressionless.

"Let's go," she said.

O:NEN

Made in the USA
Charleston, SC
08 May 2013